FRIENDS
OF ACPL

W9-BAZ-728

American Folk Tales are colorful tales of regional origin full of the local flavor and grass roots humor of special people and places. Coming from all areas of the United States, these stories provide entertaining reading material as well as insight into the customs and backgrounds of the regions from which they spring.

Distinctive color illustrations complement the text and add to the reader's enjoyment.

UNCLE DAVY LANE
MIGHTY HUNTER

by Adèle deLeeuw

illustrated by Herman B. Vestal

GARRARD PUBLISHING COMPANY
CHAMPAIGN, ILLINOIS

To Blake MacDiarmid
my young friend and neighbor

Copyright © 1970 by Adèle deLeeuw

All rights reserved. Manufactured in the U.S.A.

Standard Book Number: 8116-4023-X

Library of Congress Catalog Card Number: 79-110166

1693936

Contents

Uncle Davy Outwits a Buck

Uncle Davy Lane was the mightiest hunter in the North Carolina mountains. He said so himself and he could prove it.

"Davy," his wife said one day, "we need some meat. Why don't you leave your blacksmithin' and go and get us some venison?"

Uncle Davy looked out through the door of his shop in the barn. It was a beautiful day—too beautiful to stay inside.

"I'll bring you a deer in time for supper," he told Molly.

He ran his fingers through his long beard to comb it, and set his hunting cap on his head. He was a tall thin man. His face was the color of old leather, and he walked like a woodsman, setting his feet down without a sound.

"Good-bye, Nip," he said to his horse. "I'm just goin' over to the woods, so I won't need to ride. I'll see you toward evenin'."

His two sons, Junior and Bill, wanted to go along. "No, you just stay home with your Maw," Davy said. "You can shoe Nip and make a new rake. Then you can bring down some hay, and fix that squeaky wagon wheel. Then you'd better fetch some water. And while you're about it, be sure to pick those big stones out of the creek. When you're done you can help your Maw. I don't need company today."

He took up his trusty rifle, Bucksmasher,

which he had made himself. There wasn't a better rifle in the whole state. Then he took up his bag of bullets—he had made those, too—and started down the road toward the woods.

On the way he passed the tumbledown cabin of his old friend Sam. Sam was sitting on the front porch, rocking and smoking his corncob pipe.

"Where you goin'?" Sam demanded.

"Goin' to shoot a deer," Uncle Davy called back.

"No deer around," Sam said.

"How do you know? You haven't stirred off that porch, I'll bet, since sunup." Davy shifted Bucksmasher to his shoulder. "I'll have me a deer by evenin'," he told Sam.

When he came to the edge of the woods on Sugar Loaf Mountain, he hid behind a tree and waited. He could wait all day if he had to. A bird called from the tree above him, but otherwise it was very quiet. Uncle Davy was listening for a certain sound. He listened so hard he could almost feel his ears sticking out from his head. The sun crept higher. Uncle Davy got hot and shed his coat. He was hungry, but he had nothing to eat. He was thirsty, but he would not stir from his hiding place to find a brook.

Suddenly he heard the sound he had been listening for. There was the faintest little rustle among the leaves. Uncle Davy scarcely breathed. Rifle in hand, he clasped Bucksmasher more tightly. The sound grew a little louder. It came a little closer.

Then all at once the biggest buck Uncle Davy had ever seen jumped out of the brush. The buck was so startled to see Uncle Davy that, for a second, it stood perfectly still. Uncle Davy slowly raised his rifle.

"Oh, no, you don't!" the buck said, and took to its heels.

That startled Uncle Davy! "Oh, yes, I will!" he shouted. He was a spry man with long legs and good lungs. He ran after the buck as fast as those long legs would take him, but the buck ran still faster. They raced around and around Sugar Loaf Mountain till Uncle Davy was dizzy. Every once in a

while he'd stop long enough to load Buck-smasher and shoot, just to let the buck know he was in hot pursuit. But the buck kept going in circles around the mountain. The bullets went straight—so Uncle Davy missed every time.

It made him angry. "I'm goin' to get you yet!" he shouted.

"Try it," the buck called, as it disappeared into the woods.

It took Davy a long time to get home, he was so tired from all the running.

When he got there, Molly asked, "Where's the venison?"

"Better fry sausage meat tonight," Davy said grimly. "I found the biggest buck you ever saw, but that critter just wouldn't get shot."

Uncle Davy went back every day for a week trying to find that deer. One day he sighted the buck racing around the mountain. By now he was so angry at the buck he couldn't get to sleep at night for thinking. One night he got a bright idea.

Early next morning Davy was in his blacksmith shop. He took up his hammer and bent Bucksmasher's rifle barrel so that it had exactly the same curve as the mountain. Then he went back to Sugar Loaf and hid behind a tree.

Sure enough, after a time the same buck came running around the mountain. "Hah!" it laughed from afar. "You here again?"

With that it kicked up its heels and disappeared around a curve.

Uncle Davy took careful aim with old Bucksmasher. The bullet whizzed around the mountain in the same curve that the buck was running.

Uncle Davy put Bucksmasher under his

arm, but the bent rifle barrel poked him in the back. So he braced it against a tree and stood there, watching. First came the buck, yelling, "Where's that bullet?"

Then the bullet whizzed past, singing out, "Where's that buck?"

Uncle Davy nearly died laughing. Toward dusk the buck got less sassy, and the bullet got faster, and finally the bullet caught up with the buck.

Uncle Davy went to see what he'd finally
shot. He hung his shot bag absentmindedly
on the horn of something that was mosey-
ing by. It was a pretty thing, all bright
and silvery. When he'd finally finished
skinning the buck and trussing it up to
take home, he reached for his shot bag. It
wasn't there! He could barely see it dis-
appearing into space.

"Dod-blast it!" he shouted in dismay.

"That was the moon moseyin' by! I hung my shot bag on the horn of the moon!"

Well, that was a piece of bad luck. The bag had all his bullets in it, and all his shooting powder. He *had* to get that bag back!

He could make more bullets, for he always made his own, but the bag was something else again. Molly had sewed it for him out of a buckskin, and she had knitted the drawstrings. She wouldn't take kindly to the fact that he had been careless and lost it. What was he going to do?

On the way home he stopped and picked a bunch of wild flowers. When he gave them to Molly and showed her the buck she forgot to ask where his shot bag was.

Next night he returned to the same spot in the woods and waited. He was afraid the bag might have fallen off if the moon had been going fast. Then, just about the same time as the night before, there it came—the pretty silvery moon—with the bag hanging on its horn. Davy had never been so glad to see anything in his life.

He slipped the bag off the horn and said sternly, "Now you go on about your business, and don't try a trick like that again!" Somehow, that made him feel better.

Uncle Davy and His Hair-Raisin' Ride

Uncle Davy decided to try his luck over at Skull Camp. He had heard there was good hunting there, but he wanted to find out for himself. First, though, it took him a couple of days to straighten out the barrel of Bucksmasher.

Uncle Davy needed only a half-hour to find and shoot his first deer. He left it by the side of the path and went deeper into the woods. Then he heard another deer, and when it appeared, he shot that one, too.

"Pretty good luck today," he said out

loud. "Must be these new bullets I made. If I do say so myself, I'm the best bullet maker in North Carolina."

His luck held and he shot one deer after another. Only one or two he tried to shoot got away. Finally, there came a buck that was the biggest of the lot—a real whopper. Davy let out his breath in a soundless whistle. "If I get this one," he thought, "I'm not only the best bullet maker in the state, I'm the best shot in the whole country!"

Excitedly, he reached into his bag for another bullet.

"Dod-blast it!" he cried out loud. "They're all gone!"

How could that be? Well, he'd certainly shot plenty of deer. They were spotted all down the trail he had come.

But he couldn't let that huge buck get away. He felt in his bag again. The only thing left was a peach stone. He must have put it there the last time he ate peaches.

When he looked up, the buck had already disappeared. Well, he'd get ready for it, anyhow. It had probably gone off into the woods when he had spoken out loud. No deer would catch him doing a silly thing like that again!

Quickly he loaded his rifle with the peach stone. Then he waited. A half-hour later the buck came back, peering out from behind a leafy screen of green. Uncle Davy took aim and fired. The buck just snickered, lifted up his heels, and scampered away.

Uncle Davy stamped Bucksmasher into the ground. "Dod-blast it!" he said. Then, bit by bit, he began to feel better. After all, he had more than enough deer to take home. In fact, he had so many he couldn't handle them alone.

He strode back to his cabin. "Hitch up old Nip and the wagon," he told Junior and Bill. "You'll never believe your eyes what's waiting for us there in Skull Camp!"

By the time they'd piled the wagon high with all the deer Uncle Davy had shot, the wagon was so heavy the boys had to help Nip pull it.

"My stars!" Molly cried, when she saw the load. "We'll have deer meat to give to all the people in the valley!"

"And some to store in the smokehouse," Uncle Davy said.

"And enough buckskin for breeches for me," said Junior.

"And shirts and moccasins," said Bill.

It wasn't till three years later that Uncle Davy decided to go over to Skull Camp again. By then his supply of deer meat was running low. He was just getting ready to load Bucksmasher when he happened to see a big peach tree, loaded with the most beautiful peaches. He was standing at the edge of a cliff and the tree rose right up in front of him from the valley below.

If there was one thing Uncle Davy liked more than anything else it was peaches. He propped Bucksmasher against a rock and shinnied up that tree quicker than you could say "Davy Lane." He opened up his pocket-knife and cut himself one peach after another.

After he had eaten fifty or so, he thought he'd had enough for the time being. At least he ought to shoot a deer or two for good measure before he ate any more peaches.

Just as he was about to slide down the trunk of the tree, it moved a bit.

"Must be seein' things," Uncle Davy muttered to himself. "Trees don't move."

But it did move again, a little faster this time. "Et too many peaches," Uncle Davy said to himself in a wobbly voice. By now the tree was moving much faster, moving with Davy in it.

The whole tree had moved away from the edge of the cliff where he had been standing. Now it was gathering more speed. Uncle

Davy put his hand to his forehead. "My head's a-whirlin'!" he cried. The tree sailed along so fast that the wind began to whistle through his beard till it sounded to him like a hurricane. He tried to yell "Stop!" but his voice wouldn't come out of his throat. Uncle Davy was scared—he was scared a bright blue!

Uncle Davy hung on for dear life. Finally he got up his courage and peered down toward the ground from between his fingers. What he saw made his eyes pop! It couldn't be true, he must be imagining things!

Why, it wasn't the peach tree that was running. It was a big buck, and the tree was growing right out of its back!

That buck kept running like the wind for fifteen miles before it stopped. Uncle Davy slid down the tree and off the buck's back so fast he scorched his breeches. His knees trembled, and the wind had burned his face. His beard was all tousled, and his hunting cap was gone. It took him quite a time to trudge back to the edge of the cliff where he had left Bucksmasher. Then he limped home, more dead than alive.

"Land sakes!" Molly cried when she saw him. "What happened to you?"

He told her.

She snorted. "How come a peach tree was growin' out of a buck's back?" she asked.

"My gracious, woman, can't you figure that out for yourself? That was the buck I shot with a peach stone three years ago."

Uncle Davy and His Roostin' Horse

"Davy," his wife Molly said one day, "I'm tired of eatin' deer meat."

"I'll shoot you some turkeys," Davy offered.

"I'm tired of eatin' turkey," she said firmly. "Why don't you get me some pigeons?"

"You aim to make me a pigeon pie?"

"That I'll do, as soon as you bring the pigeons," Molly said.

Uncle Davy needed no further prodding. He picked up his musket, and filled his shot bag with drop shot. Then he harnessed Nip and rode over to Little Mountain. He had heard tell that the place was a regular pigeon

roost. He would be doing the county good by getting rid of some of the birds. Besides, if Molly wanted pigeons for pies he'd be doing her, and himself, a good turn, too.

Well, sure enough, he knew when he'd come to the right spot. The sky was dark with pigeons flying about, and it was almost as dark as night. Hundreds more were crowded on the tree branches. Uncle Davy could hardly see to set one foot in front of the other.

He tied Nip to a low tree branch and began shooting pigeons till he had all his bags full. He shot so long and so fast that his musket got hot and six inches of it melted off the end. By that time he'd had enough and went to untie Nip.

Nip had disappeared—bridle and all!

"Now, how can that be?" Uncle Davy muttered to himself. Nip must have gotten untied and wandered off, but he couldn't have moved far in this time. Uncle Davy searched over the ground; he looked under tall bushes and down into the valleys. Nip was gone.

"Nip!" he called in the gloomy, pigeon-filled air. "Nip, where are you?"

Then he heard a strange little sound. It was hard to tell where it came from. Finally he peered upward as he stood under a very tall tree.

"Dod-blast it!" he shouted. "What are you doin' up there, Nip, you old scalawag, you?"

He held his sides laughing to see Nip dangling high in the air, his legs waving in all directions. Nip started to nicker like mad.

It took quite some doing for Uncle Davy to get him down. Then Davy rode home with the bags full of pigeons. When he told Molly and the boys why he was so late, his wife

said, "Hmph! How come Nip was up in the tree?"

"Why, it so happens I had tied him to the branch of a tree that was loaded to the ground with pigeons. When they rose up, the branch went up, and so did old Nip. That's simple."

Then the boys asked, in one voice, "How did you get him down, Paw?"

Davy Lane winked one eye. "That's for you young'uns to figure out," he said.

Junior scratched his head thoughtfully. "Could be, Paw, you climbed the tree yourself to get him loose?" he asked.

"Could be," Davy chuckled.

But Bill scoffed. "Naw! Paw wouldn't climb a tree like that. Anyhow, if he had cut Nip loose, Nip would have fallen down and broke' his neck."

"What's *your* idea?" asked Junior.

Bill said slowly, "Could be, Paw, you threw a rope up and lassoed him, like they do out West, and then lowered him?"

"Could be," said Davy Lane, nodding.

Junior cried, "That wouldn't work! Paw can't throw a lasso—leastwise, he never did before."

"All right, smarty, what do *you* think?"

"*I* think," said Junior, after a long pause, "Paw waited till nightfall—'cause it *was* night when he and Nip came back. The pigeons that had flown off when Paw was shootin' came back to roost again. Then the branch Nip was on got heavy with pigeons and came down to the ground so Nip could get off. Could be, Paw?"

Davy Lane replied solemnly, "Could be, Junior."

"But which way was it?" both of the boys demanded.

Davy Lane said, "I got him down, didn't I?"

"Yes, yes!" they chorused.

"And we're both here, ain't we?"

"Sure!" they answered together.

"I can't rightly remember what I did," Uncle Davy Lane said, grinning. "But you boys sure figured out ways for me to do it if it ever happens again."

And that's all he would ever say.

Uncle Davy and the Peach-Eatin' Contest

Along about August Uncle Davy Lane went over to visit his friend Old Sam. He had a good reason for going. He knew that the two peach trees in Sam's front yard were full of peaches. And they were the most luscious peaches Davy Lane had ever tasted. The limbs were so heavy with fruit that they spread out on the ground.

"'Bout time you came around," Old Sam said. "What brings you?"

"I have a hankerin' for peaches," Davy Lane said. "Those peaches are just about

the gol-darnedest best-lookin' peaches I
ever did see. I could eat a bushel at one
sittin'."

"I could eat two bushels," said Old Sam.

"I bet I could eat more peaches than you,"
said Uncle Davy Lane.

"What do you bet?" Sam asked.

"I bet my corncob pipe against all the
peaches I can't eat."

"Hmph," said Old Sam. "What do I want
with your corncob pipe? I got one of my

own, and I like mine better. What's more, I aim to keep all the peaches you can't eat. You got to do better than that."

"All right," said Uncle Davy, after long thought. "How 'bout bettin' my Nip against your hound dog?"

"Done," said Old Sam. "I could use a horse, and Noah, my hound dog, is always roamin' over to your cabin anyhow. Where do we start?" **1693936**

"Right here. Which of these two trees do you pick to work on?"

"This one," said Sam, pointing.

"You've lost already," said Uncle Davy Lane. "I choose this one."

Old Sam scratched his head. "How are we goin' to tell which one has et the most? We can't count the peach stones—there'll be too many."

"Easy," said Uncle Davy. "Both these trees

have their branches lyin' on the ground. Isn't that so?"

"Agreed," said Old Sam, nodding.

"Well, when one of us calls quits, we'll git down and measure which tree's branches has riz up more from the ground. That's simple."

"Sounds so to me," said Old Sam. "Get set, then. One–two–three–*go!*"

With that each one took out his pocket-knife and began cutting peaches.

They started to eat about nine o'clock in the morning. By noon the peach stones covered Old Sam's front yard. By three o'clock in the afternoon there were peach stones as far as you could see. "Got enough?" Davy called over to Sam.

"Not yet." But Sam's voice sounded a little tired.

By five o'clock Uncle Davy called out, "How you doin' now, Sam?"

"I'm ready to quit, Davy. Gettin' a little heavy in the middle. How 'bout you?"

"Haven't begun yet," said Davy Lane. "But if you want to quit, it's all right by me."

They both climbed down. Uncle Davy got a big pole leaning against the cabin and brought it over to use as a measuring rod.

"Look, the branches of your tree have riz up two feet off the ground." He went over to

the tree he'd been eating in. Carefully he held up the pole against the lowest branch. "And my tree has riz up three feet! That means I et more than you. Hurray, I win!"

Old Sam said, "Much good may it do you. I've et enough peaches to last me a lifetime. And Noah's no good as a huntin' dog. So you're welcome to him."

It took Sam and Davy two weeks to shovel the peach stones off the ground and onto a nearby open field where they would be out of the way. After a while, grass grew over the pile of peach stones, and passersby thought they were Indian mounds.

You couldn't say the word "peaches" to Old Sam after that, but Uncle Davy Lane liked them as much as ever. And from then on, every year when they were ripe, Davy went over and ate all the peaches off *both* of Old Sam's trees.

Uncle Davy Is Chased by a Snake

Now there was one queer thing about Uncle Davy Lane. He was afraid of snakes. He was not only afraid of them, he hated them. Davy was always on the lookout for them when he walked through fields or woods. He had had some pretty bad experiences with them.

But Davy wasn't thinking about snakes on this particular day. He hadn't shot any deer for a long while. "It's time I got me another buck," he said one Sunday.

"It's Sunday, Davy, and you can't go shootin' on the Sabbath," his wife said.

"I've shot every day of the week 'cept Sunday, and you're not one to tell me nay," said Uncle Davy.

"This afternoon's Sunday meetin' and I aim to have you go along with me over to the church in the hollow."

"This is a prime day for deer," Uncle Davy said stubbornly. "I can smell 'em in the wind."

With that he picked up his faithful Bucksmasher and was out of the door.

He hadn't gone far in the forest when a doe crossed right in front of him. He lifted his rifle and shot it. A moment later he saw the small pointed face of a fawn peering through the leaves at the side of the path. When it spied him it leaped backward and disappeared among the trees.

Uncle Davy felt terrible. If he had known the doe had a fawn, he would never have shot it. It was a dreadful thing to do. He knew he'd never be able to sleep until he found that fawn, and took it home to care for it.

Davy propped Bucksmasher against a tree and made himself a blate—a split stick in which he put a leaf. Hunters often used them to attract deer. He hid in the laurel and blew his blate, hoping the fawn would hear it and come running. He blew and blew till he was out of breath and had to close his eyes.

When he opened them, there, in the underbrush, was a monstrous black snake! It was bigger than any snake he had ever seen in his worst nightmare. The snake had a pair of horns on its head as big as those of an antelope. It reared its head and slithered over the ground toward him.

Uncle Davy ran for his life. He ran so fast

his feet scarcely touched the path. He zig-
zagged in and out between the trees, trying
to lose the snake, but it was following him.
He stumbled over a tree root, and the snake
came even closer.

Uncle Davy flung off his shirt and threw
it backward, hoping it would land on the
snake's head, but when he turned to look,

he saw that the snake had slithered right over it. Those horns were immense! Whoever heard of a snake with horns? Nobody would believe him . . . but there it was, a snake with horns, and it was gaining on him.

Uncle Davy ran so fast his breeches fell off. But he kept on running in his underpants. The snake slithered faster, too, and Uncle Davy fairly flew over the ground. Puffing and blowing, he ran right on past

his own cabin. He was scared a bright green.

He hid behind a tree, trying to get his breath back. Then he heard Molly calling.

"Davy! Davy Lane! What are you doin', hidin' out there?"

"Where's that snake?"

"What snake?"

"That buck-horned snake that was chasin' me."

She laughed. "I told you not to go shootin'

on a Sunday. There isn't any snake. I been sittin' right here by the window and nothin' went by, 'cept you, and *you* went by like a flash."

"I tell you, there *is* a snake, a snake with horns."

She came toward him. "My land, what are you doin' in your underpants? Where's your shirt and breeches?"

He looked sheepish. "Along the path somewhere, I guess." Now that Molly was with him he felt a little better. "That snake's somewhere hereabouts and I've got to find it."

Together they walked back toward the cabin. Uncle Davy peered under the bench that sat beneath the oak tree. He looked in the well. He searched behind a huge rock.

"Oh, look!" Molly said. Davy jumped a mile.

"Where is it?" he shouted.

"There! That cute little fawn peerin' round the corner of the cabin! Now I do wonder where it came from. It must be lookin' for its Maw."

Davy cried, "Why, that's the fawn I saw in the woods!" And he told Molly how he had shot the doe without knowing she had a fawn with her.

Molly looked wise. "That wasn't a snake,

then," she said firmly. "That was the Devil. He was chasin' you for shootin' on a Sunday. . . . And where's Bucksmasher and your shot bag?"

"They're in the woods. The boys can git them and my clothes tomorrow."

Maybe Molly was right, Davy thought. He was mighty relieved to know it wasn't a snake—only the Devil looking like a snake.

Davy said loudly, "One thing's certain. I won't ever go shootin' again on a Sunday."

He and Molly walked toward the fawn, trembling beside the cabin and looking at them with its big brown eyes.

"Goin' to be right busy from now on," said Uncle Davy Lane, "workin' at my blacksmithin' and raisin' that fawn so it won't miss its Maw."

MEET THE AUTHOR

Adele deLeeuw says "children's stories are a natural occupation for me." When Adele and her sister, Cateau, were small girls, they entertained each other telling stories. Storytelling became a career when the deLeeuws put their talents to work in the Plainfield, New Jersey Public Library. Their story hours were so popular that Miss deLeeuw converted from storytelling to story writing. Her published books now number 58 and have been transcribed into Braille. Her short stories have appeared in more than a hundred magazines. Her poems have been set to music, sung on the radio, and recorded. *Uncle Davy Lane: Mighty Hunter* is Miss deLeeuw's 11th book for Garrard.

MEET THE ARTIST

Herman B. Vestal loves both painting and the sea. Before studying art at the National Academy of Design and Pratt Institute, he went to sea in the merchant marine. During World War II he served in the Coast Guard as a combat artist. His assignments included recording the Normandy landing and the invasion of Iwo Jima. Today his interest in the sea continues through his hobby — sailboat racing. Primarily a book illustrator, Mr. Vestal also enjoys doing watercolors and is a member of the American Watercolor Society. Mr. Vestal, his wife and son live in Little Silver, New Jersey.